A CRADLEY ALBUM

Written and compiled by Peter Barnsley

Two Gates Publications, 35 Meadowcroft, West Hagley
1994

Printed by Reliance Printing Works, Halesowen, West Midlands

A Cradley Album

ISBN 0 9512 365 2 0

First Published 1994

Introduction

Since the publication of the first collection of old photographs of Cradley nearly two years ago, many more such photographs have been shown to me. People very kindly took the trouble to look out so many old post-cards, family portraits and casual snapshots that it soon became apparent that there would be enough material for a second collection. So here it is. I can only hope that it will be as well received as the first.

The appeal of old photographs is based partly on curiosity, and partly on the common human emotion of nostalgia (of all longings, the one that must remain forever unsatisfied). To crave for the return of past times – often of times beyond the reach of our own memories – is a familiar experience for most of us. There can be few – if any – people now living who can remember Drews Holloway as it appears on page three of this booklet, but there will probably be equally few who do not wish it could be like that again.

But nostalgia selects the evidence. There is always another story. In 1932 (which is about half-way through the period covered by these photographs) Cradley's vicar, the Reverend Ernest Toulouse, appealing for contributions to the St. Peter's restoration fund, wrote: "Cradley is a large industrial parish in the Black Country. The people are all poor . . ." He was overstating the case. Nevertheless, the collection of £98 8sh. 6d. at High Town Ragged School's Anniversary in the same year was thought to be very gratifying – " . . in view of the depressed conditions prevailing in the parish." And at the quarterly meeting of the Worcestershire branches of the British Legion that was held at Stourbridge Town Hall, the Cradley Branch reported that of 400 ex-servicemen in Cradley, about 300 were unemployed. Nor was it always fun to be young. In October 1933, the Elementary Education Sub-committee of Worcestershire County Council reported that all Cradley's schoolchildren had been examined by a school doctor, and that 257 of them were suffering from malnutrition. Inevitably, the clammy hands of the Depression squeezed many lives in Cradley.

By all means, long for the old days. Good times were certainly had – but not by all.

Photographers

Where I have known the name of a photographer – or of the firm that employed him – I have given the appropriate credit. Where I have been unable to discover the name of the photographer, I have so indicated. The absence of any acknowledgement of any kind below a photograph indicates that I took it myself.

Dates and Faces

As with the previous collection, some of the photographs reproduced here can be placed accurately in time (in one or two cases even to the day); with others – including, I have to admit, some of my own – it has been a matter of deduction and, sometimes, intelligent (one hopes) guesswork.

The other, greater, problem has been to identify people – being able to put names to faces gives additional interest to a photograph. I have taken as much care as possible to identify people correctly – and I am grateful to all those whom I have pestered to ransack their memories of fifty or sixty years ago or more to help me in that task. If mistakes have been made (and human memory is fallible) I accept full responsibility for them.

Corrections

It is a reasonable assumption that many of those who buy this booklet will have been purchasers of the previous one. It therefore seems a good idea to correct here mistakes that I now know to have been made in the earlier publication.

First, I was mistaken in assuming that no postcards of Cradley were published after the Second World War; two such cards appear in this collection. Second, the photograph of the gardens below St. Peter's Church was taken about fifteen years earlier than I thought (this error was corrected in the reprints of the booklet). Third, I inexplicably gave Charles H. Clewes the initials (T.M.) of his son, Matthew ('Moggy') Clewes. Fourth, majority opinion holds that I was wrong in naming Mary Gill as one of the women on the doorstep in New Street. (See p. 40).

In two other matters, I was only half right. I stated that the Anvil Yard was demolished for reasons of public health. This was only one of the reasons, the other being that the road needed widening. The Ministers of both Health and Public Transport were consulted before the demolition (which was carried out by Joe Tate's men in the late summer of 1931).

Finally, I was correct in stating that John Wilson, the local Liberal M.P., had at one time crossed the floor of the House of Commons. But he did not cross from the Conservative benches. He was originally elected as a Liberal but joined the breakaway Liberal Unionists (who allied themselves with the Conservatives over the Home Rule Bill). Mr. Wilson subsequently rejoined the Liberals.

Acknowledgments

It would be impossible to mention everyone who has helped me in some way or other during the preparation of this booklet. Some have provided photographs, some information – and others have made enquiries for me or simply suggested other possible sources of information.

I must mention in particular Eric and Betty Smith whose help – as with the previous collection – has been invaluable. And for his work in restoring old photographs, I am again indebted to Barry Freeman – in particular for the excellent job he did in joining two negatives to produce the photograph that appears across the centre pages. For the second time, too, I am grateful for architectural information from Paul Gibbons – this time in respect of Colman Hill House.

My thanks also to the following (if I have omitted anyone, I can assure them that it is because of my lack of organisation – not of appreciation): John Billingham, Edna, Ruth and Jim Blackwell, Margaret Bowater, Paul Burgess, Maud Chapman, Margaret Clifton, Norman and Hazel Clifton, Maurice Cole, Bruce Cooley, Jack Deeley, Bess Downton, Muriel Downton, Eileen Forrest, Mabel Gopsill, Betty Griffin, Jill Guest, Ethel Hall, Brian Harper, Molly Harper, Julie Hipkiss, Rex and Sheila Jones, Alice Meredith, Dennis Moore, Ken and Roma Oakley, John Pearson, Sandra Phipps, Michael Rosser, Geoff Russell, Edna Smith, Hubert Southall, Elsie Stevens, Norman Stevens, David Tate, Arthur Taylor, Marie Trevis, Mary Tromans, Ernie Walton, Major-General J. A. Ward-Booth, Geoff Willetts, Olive Willetts, Geoff Woodall and Edna Yates.

I also wish to acknowledge the help of the staff of the Reference Section of Stourbridge Library, where the back numbers of the *County Express* have again provided much useful information.

The details of the closure of Beech Tree Colliery are taken from an article by Christine Cartwright in the *Sunday Mercury* of 14th September, 1958. The details about the demolition of the colliery stack are taken from the *Express and Star* (which also included a photograph of the stack as it collapsed).

Peter Barnsley,
October, 1994.

Front Cover Photographs

Top: Annie Tate (left) who, as the second Mrs. Herbert Cox, was to be Halesowen's Mayoress from November 1938 to November 1940. Miss Tate also appears in the lower photograph on page 14. The young lady on the right is a Miss Jones. The photograph is probably early Edwardian.

(Photo: George Redding, Stourbridge).

Middle: Posing for a photograph to commemorate the Coronation of King George V on 23rd June 1911. The *Round of Beef* and its neighbouring buildings are easily recognised, but to the modern eye the scene does seem to be missing something. A photographer who tried to take such a photograph now, would have a two-mile queue of traffic in both directions before he finished.

Standing in the doorway of the nearest shop is Frank Southall who had the unusual history for a Cradley grocer – or any grocer for that matter – of having been ordained as a Methodist minister. He remained in the ministry for only four years – first at Thorne in Yorkshire, and then in Tavistock in Devonshire – before returning to Cradley and entering the family business. During the 1914-18 war, he ran not only his own business but those of his younger brothers, Wilf and Walter, who were in the services. He died, unmarried, in 1932 at the age of 48.

(Photographer unidentified).

Bottom: Jesse Dunn outside his grocery store in Two Gates Lane (see page 10).

Drews Holloway

Photo: Luxia

The above postcard shows Drews Holloway, photographed from its junction with Belle Vale. The card is dated 1906. Note the glimpse of the weir at the bottom left of the photograph. The stream that passes under the road was dammed originally to drive a water wheel at Drews Forge, which was on the other side of the road. In its later days, at least, Drews Forge made spades and shovels; it was owned by the Bache family, and was powered by a gas engine. The Holloway Pool (see below) is behind the wall on the left.

Photographer unidentified

The Holloway Pool, created by the damming of the stream, as it looked in the Edwardian age (the card was posted on 5th August 1909). Kingfishers were known to nest in its banks, and there was a rowing-boat moored at its side. But few people can now remember its attractions.

Photographer unidentified

Drews Holloway, looking down from its junction with Colman Hill. The house is still there – though no longer isolated. The Witley Colliery spoil bank is visible in the background, to the right of the trees. The card was posted in 1905 by a Louie Burke of *Park House,* Cradley, who wrote, *"This is a photo of our favourite road for walks . . . . . . ".*

Photographer unidentified

The junction of Colman Hill and Drews Holloway. The card was posted in 1922. The house – *Hillcrest* – was built by the chain manufacturer, Frank Sykes, probably about the turn of the century. It might have been the first house in Cradley to have electricity; Mr. Sykes installed his own generator and wiring (the wiring caused consternation to MEB electricians when the house was rewired many years later). *Hillcrest* was later owned by Alf Ryland, a Cradley Heath manufacturer, and in 1930 it was bought by William Blackwell. Jim and Ruth Blackwell lived there until 1964, when the house was demolished as part of the scheme for the proposed A456 relief road. In September 1994, the Local Authority decided to abandon the proposal.

Photographer unidentified

Showing Drews Holloway with a more modern appearance – Drews Holloway South, The Drive, a telephone pole and motor cars – this card is postmarked 1936, but the photograph could well have been taken a few years earlier. The drive on the left leads to Holloway House (once known as Essington House).

Photographer unidentified

From Colman Hill, looking uphill, the above photograph of Drews Holloway was probably taken in the 1930's. The houses are still there, except for Clyndon House in the background, which was once the family home of Caleb Woodhouse.

Beecher Road

Photo: Charles F. Everitt

Beecher Road, looking southwards towards Beecher Street and Alma Street. The postcard was sent by someone named Hilda who lived in Beecher Road; it is postmarked August 7th, 1912. The house on the right is now the Vicarage.

Photographer unidentified

Another view of the same row of houses in Beecher Road. The date of the photograph is unknown but it was probably taken at about the same time as – or perhaps a little later than – the top photograph.

Two Gates

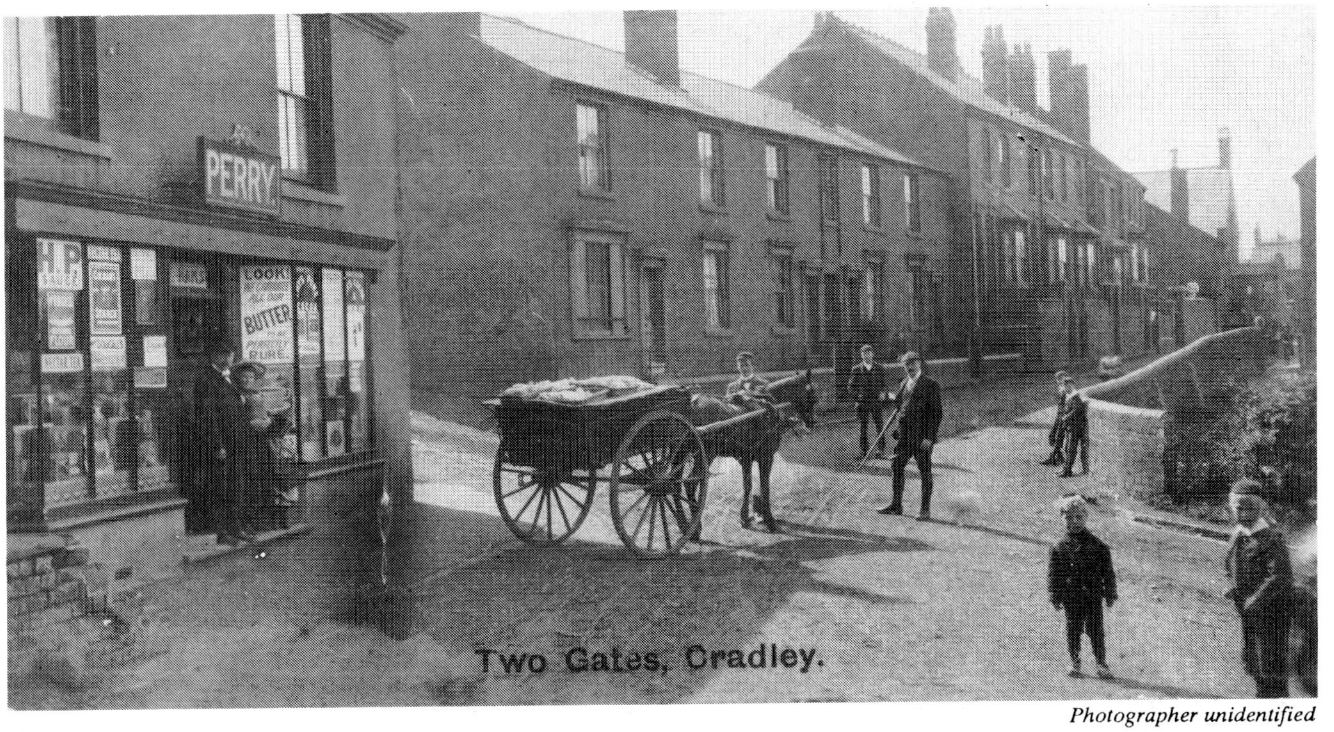

Photographer unidentified

Two Gates as it looked in about 1904. The man standing in the shop doorway is believed to be its proprietor, Harry Perry, with Mrs. Perry and one of their two daughters. Mr. Perry died in Norton in January 1930, aged 68. One daughter, Irene, grew up to marry another local grocer, Walter Southall. Expert opinion – after much debate – has decided that the imposing figure with the shotgun is probably George Oliver, from the Talbot Hotel.

Photographer unidentified

The Vine Inn, Two Gates in or about 1927. Standing in front of the Vine are (left to right): Joe Clifton, Isaac Taylor Jnr., David Taylor, Vernon Clifton, William Taylor, Isaac Taylor Snr., Harry Taylor Snr. (the licensee), Alban Hill, John Taylor, Ben Pearson (?), Harry Taylor Jnr., and Wilf Bowen (?). The lady looking through the ground floor window on the left is believed to be Kate Taylor.

Photographer unidentified

Photographer unidentified

Bill Billingham (above), the son of the original owner, outside Billingham's General Store in Two Gates. The store, which stood opposite the Ragged School, closed in or about 1968.

The Village Nuts, clockwise from the top left, are Cliff Willetts – later to be Mayor of Halesowen, George Billingham, Walter Hough, John Taylor and Vernon Harris. 'Nuts' was presumably used in its Edwardian sense of swells or dandies. The photograph is post-Edwardian – but not by many years.

Photo: G. Robson, Blackheath

Two Gates Ragged School Sunday School, winners of the Woodhouse Shield for Scripture Knowledge in 1935. *Back row (left to right):* Millie Taylor, Jill Hipkiss, Elsie Crampton, Gladys Garratt, Annie Pearson, Daisy Homer, Minnie Cooper, Gladys Griffin, Mona Brittain, Gladys Cooper, Bella Payne, Mary Griffin, Kate Malpass. *Middle row:* James Adams, Emmie Boxley, Alice Evans, Cliff Willetts, Joseph Hodgetts, Edwin Bird, Doris Wood, Rose Bache, Enoch Growcott. *Front row:* Olive Stokes, Marion Wellings, Elsie Griffin, Pearl Boxley, Peggy Williams, Bill Hipkiss, Eric Hill, Clifford Pegg, Alice Taylor, Renee Billingham, Ada James, Rose Boxley.

The view (above) from Two Gates in 1968 when the ground was being cleared for the Tanhouse flats. The first row of houses marks the line of part of Park Road and Park Lane. The pond that is just visible in the middleground on the right was filled in shortly after the photograph was taken.

The photograph below was taken probably about ten years earlier from alongside that pond, looking towards Two Gates. The pond was said to mark the site of an old claypit – the clay being dug for the brickworks of Harper and Moore in Park Road.

Photographer unidentified

The grocery store of W. and J. Dunn in Two Gates Lane in about 1912. From left to right: William Dunn, Jesse Dunn, John Butterworth, Edgar Dunn, Irene Dunn, Reg Dunn, Florence Dunn (with Elsie Dunn), Betsy Dunn, Louise (Griffiths?). Reg Dunn, a vice-president of Worcestershire County Cricket Club, now lives in retirement in Churchill. The shop, now demolished, stood just above the *Round of Beef.*

Photographer unidentified

From about the same period as the top photograph: Furlong Lane, with Spring Street leading off on the right.

Photographer unidentified

The above scene suggests Thomas Hardy's Wessex rather than the Black Country. But the haymakers in the photograph are not Dorsetshire peasants. They are (from left to right): William Stevens, his wife Mary, and his sons Joe Stevens and William Henry Stevens. The photographer was standing near the site of the present Tanhouse flats, looking towards Colley Gate.

In the background of the photograph, which was taken in about 1914, are the house of Richard Green (far left) whose land is now part of Greenways, and the group of buildings that included the tanhouse that gave its name to Tanhouse Lane. Joe Stevens is still remembered from his later years as a coal-haulier. Most of Cradley's male pensioners remember riding – as schoolboys – on his horse-drawn cart.

Photo: George Flavell

From about the same time – a photograph of George Ashmore's horse and cart in the tanyard. John Ashmore (George's son) holds the reins.

Colley Lane Boys' School Gardening Class

Photo: George Holdsworth, Holmfirth

Headmaster James Homer (third from left) and Walter Hodgetts (fourth from left) supervise a gardening class at Colley Lane Boys' School in 1910. The land is now part of the school playing field. The ground of Colley Gate Cricket Club lay behind the fence on the right, and the land behind the hedge on the left belonged to the Fox family of *The Elms,* which stood next to the Girls' School.

With reference to the land lying behind the hedge, the report of the Sites and Buildings Sub-committee that was presented to Worcestershire Education Committee in October 1931 makes interesting reading:

> "... *After making exhaustive enquiries for a suitable site for the erection of a senior council school at Cradley, the sub-committee has come to the conclusion that the best site is one consisting of about 3,388 square yards belonging to Miss Fox, and on which her residence stands, together with about three and a half acres of land immediately adjoining, which belongs to Cradley Liberal Club. The sub-committee considers that it is very desirable that a site should be acquired for future use, and accordingly they propose to ask the district valuer to value the land on behalf of the Local Education Authority* ... "

Later, of course, the Education Committee decided to build the original 'senior council school' on what is now the site of Cradley High School, and not behind *The Elms* and the Liberal Club. All things considered, it was undoubtedly a wise decision.

The Verger

Photographer unidentified

Still wearing the forthright look of the blacksmith he once was, Charlie Worton was verger and sexton of St. Peter's for 45 years until his death in May 1926 when he was nearly 70 years old. He was also for many years the caretaker of the Church School.

When performing his Church duties, Charlie invariably wore his top hat with the gold band, and his blue frock coat with red facings. The churchyard was known during his tenure of office as 'Charlie's Park' – and by all accounts he ruled over it in a fiercely autocratic manner. The photograph was probably taken in the Edwardian period.

Builders and Sunday School Teachers

Photographer unidentified

The workmen of J. M. Tate and Son, who built the houses in Drews Holloway South, Cradley's first council houses, in 1921. Photographed in front of some of their handiwork are: *Back row (left to right):* A. Beasley, Joe Knowles, Harry Forrest, Harold Beasley, A. Cornock. *Middle row:* Bert Cook, Walter Cornock, Basil Glazebrook, Nathan Brettell, Ben Clifton, Joe Knowles Jnr., Frank Knowles, William Jackson, Reuben Rudge. *Front row:* Harry Chapman, Walter Oliver, Joe Trickett (with unidentified boy), Hartley Clifton, Fred(?) Reece, W. Morton.

Photo: C. Wilkes Green, Bromsgrove

Joe and David Tate appear in their other guise as Sunday School teachers in this Providence Methodist group photographed (probably during a Sunday School treat) in Caleb Roper's nine-acre field at a spot roughly where Parkside Road now lies. *Back row (left to right):* Caleb Worton, David Tate, Herbert Edge, Fred Willetts, Herbert Cox, Enoch Pugh, Walter Cornock, Edgar Dunn, Frank Bloomer, Bert Hickman, Bert Adams. *Middle row:* Carrie Roper, Annie Newton, Liza Grove, Daisy Edge, Hilda Roper, Florrie Grazebrook, Hilda Worton, Annie Tate, Florrie Gill, Cathy Cook. *Front row:* Clarrie Woodhouse, Wilf Homer, Sam Gauden, Joe Tate, William Blackwell, Bert Roper, Francis Hickman.

Part of the Drews Holloway south estate can be seen behind Caleb Worton. The chimney stack between Fred Willetts and Herbert Cox is presumably that of Drews Forge.

Colley Gate

Photographer unidentified

The above postcard, which is postmarked September 1922, shows Colley Gate looking eastwards towards Windmill Hill. Of the visible buildings, only that on the corner of Maple Tree Lane (with its sun-blind down), remembered by most people nowadays as Errington's, has been demolished. But behind the trees on the right were three detached houses that have now gone – those of Richard Green (out of shot on the cameraman's right), Frank Hipkiss, whose gateway is visible opposite Maple Tree Lane, and Thomas Homer. The old Vicarage – the first gateway on the right – is still standing.

Photo: Landscape View Publishers, Market Harborough

About forty years later, the same stretch of road looking westwards. Only the old British Legion building, which is just visible beyond the *Talbot Hotel* and its former malthouse, is no longer standing.

102 Windmill Hill

Photographer unidentified

Number 102 Windmill Hill stands on part of what was once a larger plot of land that filled the angle of Furlong Lane and Windmill Hill. This larger plot was itself part of a still larger piece of land called Colman Field. From surviving documents it is possible to trace some stages in the history of this plot from as far back as 1748. In October of that year, the Court Baron of Cradley Manor admitted one Elizabeth Tompson to possession of the land on the death of her father, whose only child she was. This was done "*. . . according to the custom of the said manor.*"

The Toys Connection

The name Colman Field occurs again in an agreement of February 1776, in which William Toys, a malt-mill maker, agreed to sell to Thomas Raybould, a scythesmith of Kingswinford, five pieces of land "*. . all which said five parcels of land adjoin together and are bounded by . . . a lane called the Furlong Lane and the turnpike road leading from Stourbridge to Halesowen.*" Some at least of this land had been acquired by Toys from his father, John Toys, and some of it from the estate of one Thomas Milward but unfortunately no plan survives to identify the different pieces of land. The Toys name survives of course, in Toys Lane.

As part of this transaction, William Toys reserved the right (until 1780) to work the brick-kiln, which he had erected on part of the land, and to get clay out of that part of the land marked out for the purpose. He was to pay Raybould a guinea (£1.05) a year for this concession.

The Moles

Eventually, the property was acquired – and possibly added to – in two separate transactions (1790 and 1814) by a blacksmith and victualler named Daniel Mole.

In January 1840, Daniel Mole settled the property on his son – also named Daniel and also a blacksmith. The latter died in December 1848, only six days after making his will, which was probably

Windmill Hill in the 1960's. Number 102 is in the foreground on the extreme left. The hanging 'Philips' sign marks the property as being then the premises of Andrews and Ennis.

The top part of Windmill Hill on a dull day in January 1961. The conversion of the houses into shops was just about to begin.

made because of his expected demise. In his will, the property was described as " . . *freehold garden . . . adjoining the turnpike road from Stourbridge to Halesowen.*" (The name Windmill Hill still did not appear). He bequeathed the land to his wife Frances.

What you might call the modern history of the property began in October 1853 when Frances Mole sold it to Thomas Laister, a maltster of Ivy House Farm, Quinton. The property was still described as " . . . *all that plot or parcel of garden ground* . . . " but it must have been Laister who built on the *"garden ground"* the house that is now 102, Windmill Hill.

Thomas Laister was still living in July 1892 when he sold the mineral rights in the property to the colliery owners William Hartley King and Charles King for £600. By this time, that part of the property that fronted onto Furlong Lane had been sold, and the building seen on the left of the photograph on the previous page had been built – a building still remembered by many as a branch of the Midland Bank run by Mr. McIntosh.

Twentieth Century

In 1912, number 102 Windmill Hill was sold to John Sidaway by Thomas Laister's two spinster sisters who were still living at Ivy House (the 'Farm' had been dropped) in Quinton. They had presumably inherited number 102 on their brother's death.

John Sidaway, a timber merchant's manager, lived there with his wife, Clara (the lady in the photograph) until 1921 when he sold it to the decorator Sam Gauden, whose shop it was until 1956. Sam Gauden sold it to the radio and television engineer Frederick Andrews who died in 1975. The premises are now owned by Bruce Cooley, whose insurance office is situated just above them. Only the appearance of the lower storey has been changed; two large shop windows now cover most of its length.

Two Churchmen . . . .

Joe Bloomer was nineteen years old on the outbreak of the First World War. He served on the Western Front, and suffered a shrapnel wound while serving with an artillery battery (in which his task had been to look after the horses). Though the wound was a comparatively minor one, it was enough to put him in hospital. He was eventually posted back to England, where he volunteered for the Royal Flying Corps.

Joe Bloomer was demobilised from the Royal Air Force (which replaced the RFC) in 1919, and returned to his pre-war trade as carpenter and cabinet-maker. Before enlisting, he had served an apprenticeship with Stringer's of Stourbridge. After the war, he worked in Cradley – first for J. A. Meredith, and then for Joe Tate. Finally, he joined Maddocks and Walford, a Birmingham firm that provided wooden fittings and carvings for Roman Catholic churches. The Catholic connection was ironic; Joe was a pillar of Cradley St. Peter's, which church he served as bell-ringer, chorister and churchwarden.

After his marriage to Gertrude Beasley (whose father, Caleb, was also a cabinet-maker) Joe lived at Park View, Two Gates, until his death in his fifty-first year in March 1946. He left no children; the altar of the side-chapel in St. Peter's was made by him in memory of his son, Raymond, who died in infancy.

Photographer unidentified

Joe Bloomer in the uniform of the Royal Flying Corps.

★ ★ ★ ★

The Reverend J. V. Ward-Booth came to Cradley as a curate in June 1927. He contributed more to parish life than the fulfilment of his clerical duties. He was an enthusiastic member of St. Peter's Drama Group for whom he frequently appeared on stage, and he wrote and appeared in comic sketches at carnivals and concerts. He played cricket for St. Katherine's – but when St. Katherine's played St. Peter's, the curate opted to play for the mother church. He was punished for his desertion; he got a duck.

After failing to become an army chaplain because of his eyesight (he had been temporarily blinded during the battle of Jutland) he eventually left Cradley in November 1931 to become curate of St. Saviour's in Hagley. At a farewell tea party and entertainment in the Church School, there were speeches and presentations; and songs, dances and recitations by the pupils. A popular curate was given a worthy send-off.

Tony Ward-Booth was born during his father's curacy in Cradley but – disappointingly – the birth did not take place in the parish. Otherwise, he would surely have become the highest-ranking army officer to be born in Cradley. The future commander of 16 Parachute Brigade, Director of the Army Air Corps, and GOC West Midland District – Major-General Anthony Ward-Booth, still has a few lingering childhood memories of Cradley. *"My great joy was to be allowed to go with the coalman on his rounds. I was sat on the cart-horse, and to this day can remember the smell of horse and leather, not to mention coal. I also used to visit the small chainmakers with my father, and was fascinated by the furnaces, the leather aprons, the long tongs for handling the chain, and the hard-working figures quenching their thirsts with cold tea from Corona pop bottles".*

Photographer unidentified

Rev. J. V. Ward-Booth and his son, Tony in the back garden of their home – 52 Colley Lane.

A Baptist . . . .

Photo: K. J. Whitlock & Sons, Birmingham

Charles Hodgetts Clewes died at his home in Park Road in December 1923, in the parish where he was born and had lived all his life. Until shortly before his death he had been active both in his private affairs and in his public duties. In business, he was a manufacturer of rope, twine and bags. In public life, he had been chairman of the old School Board, and became the first chairman of the School Managers' Committee (the supervisory body for Colley Lane and Netherend Schools). He was a county councillor for twenty years, and was generally credited with having persuaded the council to buy the land on which Colley Lane School was built. He was the first president of Cradley Liberal Club, which position he held for the rest of his life. He became a magistrate in 1905, and sat on the Stourbridge Bench until shortly before his death (Cradley was then in the Stourbridge Police Division). Charles Clewes was a Baptist for sixty-eight years, and was senior deacon at Halesowen Baptist Church. He was the first Cradley man to be elected chairman of Halesowen Rural District Council. And he was, withal, a genial and popular man.

. . . . . And a Few Crusted Characters

Photographer unidentified

The Oakley Brothers' sports ground in Banners Lane on a summer's evening in the 1930's. The annual sports day is over, and a group of officials pauses for a photograph. Facing the setting sun are *(left to right):* Tommy Nock, Unidentified, Bill Harbach, Unidentified, James Oakley, Norman Clewitt (?), General Mole, A. E. Hackett (who was the official starter), Albert Worton, Harry Cooper, Unidentified. The man raising his hat in the background must also remain unidentified.

Belle Vale is concealed in the ravine behind them, and the row of trees in the background is lining the drive that leads to Corngreaves Hall.

Oakleys' Works

Saturday 16th June, 1928. Oakley Brothers' 1927 *Sentinel* steam lorry (made in Shrewsbury) decorated for the Cradley Carnival, in which it carried a jazz band dressed as golliwogs. The band included Fred Webb, the leader, on drums, and Ken Newton on alto-saxophone. The man on the extreme right is Bill Shaw.

Casting a mould at Oakley's in 1937 or 1938. *Left to right:* Unidentified, Sid Rose, Ted Cartwright, Fred Raybould.

(None of the photographers has been identified)

The firm's brand new (1933) *Albion* six-tonner, about to start its maiden trip to W. T. Henley's in Gravesend. The workmen, left to right, are: Joe Worton (warehouseman), Teddy Morris (machine shop), Fred Webb (machine shop) and the driver, Edwin Isaiah Geary (familiarly known as 'Saiah).

Mr. Geary and his lorry had a remarkable escape on the 25th November, 1944. As they came through New Cross, London, on their way back from Gravesend, they were caught in the blast from a V2 rocket that landed on a nearby Woolworth's store. It was the worst V2 disaster of the war; over 160 people were killed. The blast blew the cab off the lorry, leaving Isaiah Geary completely exposed but unscratched. Steering out of the chaos, he stopped to buy a pair of goggles, and drove stoically home. There was no tarpaulin on the lorry at the time, and when it was unloaded in Cradley, gloves, scarves, purses and other personal belongings were found in the back of the lorry – blown there by the blast.

Cradley's Prize Band

Photographer unidentified

James Robins (1875–1959) the cornettist who founded the Cradley XLCR Band. The photograph was taken in his earlier playing days.

Photographer unidentified

Sarah Robins outside the family shop (now demolished) in Banners Street, probably in the 1920's.

Anyone with an imaginative cast of mind could probably still hear – in quiet moments in the right places in Cradley – the faint, lingering echoes of music-making long ago. The window panes of St. Katherine's still perhaps gently reverberate to the closing notes of Percy Smith's bass solos in the choir's first performance of Stainer's *Crucifixion* in March 1932; the piping choruses of the Sunday School scholars who sang in Gertrude Sullens' children's operetta *The Pierrette Princess* in January 1931 can doubtless still be discerned by the suggestible listener sitting quietly in the Overend Mission; and the syncopated rhythms of the Blue Ricardo Dance Band doubtless still shake the dust on the rafters of the school hall in Colley Lane, where many dances were held between the wars.

There used to be no shortage of music in Cradley: sacred music in churches and chapels; Victorian and Edwardian ballads at various concerts and dinners; operettas, staged for the most part by one or other of the chapels; and modern dance music reflecting the growing popularity of ballroom dancing. But the musicians whose music echoes loudest down the years, whose confident, brazen notes must still ricochet among the chimney pots above the streets where they marched, are the bandsmen of Cradley Excelsior (XLCR) Brass Band.

Jim Robins

The XLCR band was founded, led and inspired by the diminutive cornettist, Jim Robins (he stood scarcely an inch or two over five feet) who, with his wife Sarah, kept a little tobacconist's and confectionery at the bottom of Banners Street. Jim Robins was also a freelance insurance agent, and he collected hire-purchase payments on behalf of Aherne's, a tailor's shop at Lye Cross. At one time he had conducted the pit orchestra in the *Royal Theatre* in Cradley Heath. He had a quick temper and an autocratic manner, but without him there would have been no Cradley band.

Engagements

The band was founded in October 1924, its patron and president being Charles Willetts who allowed the band free use of the canteen at his Colonial Works in Overend Road for rehearsals.

Instruments, uniforms and music were bought with money from fees that the band received for its engagements. On the day that the bandsmen first wore their uniforms – in April 1926 – a special celebration took place at *Fair View,* Charles Willetts' home in Drews Holloway. Light refreshments were served; A. E. Hackett, Chairman of the Committee, made a congratulatory speech; Jim Robins was presented with a folding, silver-mounted ebony baton (paid for mostly by the bandsmen); the band had its photograph taken; and Richard Green and Frank Hipkiss respectively proposed and seconded a vote of

Photographer unidentified

Charles Willetts, 1860-1951

thanks to Charles Willetts. The band played a few selections, and then marched off to parade round the parish. On its way, it stopped periodically to play, and attracted many favourable comments on both its music and its dress.

The band was immediately popular in Cradley, and was to be heard at a variety of functions and ceremonies, both indoors and outdoors. And its fame soon spread beyond Cradley. At the Annual Meeting and Dinner of the band at the Colonial Works in January 1929, Mr. Hackett pointed out that in 1928, the band had had twenty-eight engagements *" . . . not only in Cradley but as far afield as Dudley, Stourbridge, Cookley, Tenbury and Belbroughton."* (Not far afield by modern standards, but this was long before motorways and widespread car ownership).

The band regularly graced the Homer Hill bandstand, which had been erected as part of Cradley's War Memorial in 1928, and it was probably because of the band's pleas that a roof was erected over the bandstand which, in its original form, was unroofed.

The band's repertoire (apart from hymns and sacred music on appropriate occasions) probably consisted mainly of marches – but the quartet from the band that formed part of the entertainment at a British Legion smoking concert in the Conservative Club in March 1929, presumably played something neither sacred nor regimental but more suited to the occasion.

Prize Band

In June 1929, Cradley Carnival Committee decided to hold a brass band contest as part of that year's carnival festivities. Before the day of the carnival arrived, there was a minor disagreement about the capacity of the bandstand. Jim Robins was told that, allowing two feet per player, there would be enough room on the bandstand for each of the competing bands. He disagreed. He argued that he could not get twenty-three players, with music stands and conductor, comfortably on the bandstand because players of the larger instruments took up much more space than two feet per man. (It is possible that the band was larger in its earlier days, or perhaps it was augmented for the contest, but Brian Harper, (Jim Robins grandson,) who played in the band in the 1940's, recalls that there were usually about sixteen bandsmen). Jim Robins won the argument. He proposed that the bands should play on the grass of the recreation ground, and this suggestion was adopted.

On Carnival Day, only four bands took part in the contest (Cradley, Woodgate, Gornal Wood and another whose name is not recorded) but it was nonetheless a serious competition. The adjudicator, Mr. W. H. Fairhurst, had travelled from Manchester, and the famous instrument-making firm of Boosey and Hawkes had presented four medals to be awarded to the best instrumentalists.

All four bands played the test piece, *Souvenirs of the Opera,* and Mr. Fairhurst awarded the contest – and the £7 prize money – to the Cradley Band. Two of the medals also went to Cradley bandsmen: A. Bowen (tenor horn) and Howard Robins (trombone).

Cradley XLCR thus became a prize band.

Busy Programme

Whether or not because of its new status, the band found itself with a busy programme ahead. Its engagements included a Sunday concert on the bandstand at Homer Hill; an appearance at a charity cricket match on the ground behind the Talbot Hotel; and a sacred concert on a Sunday evening in July in a field by Butcher's Lane – " *. . kindly lent by Mr. Thomas Webster for the benefit of Mr. Fred Shaw who met with a serious accident . . while following his employment."*

The band also appeared at Oakley Brothers' Recreation Ground in Banners Lane for the firm's first annual sports day. It was at the ground from 3 p.m. until 9 p.m. " *. . . and played some very good selections."*

Dinners

To celebrate its busy season – and its crowning achievement of 'prize' status – the band held a celebration dinner at the *White Lion* in Windmill Hill in November. At this dinner, Jim Robins said that he attributed the band's success to the fact that all the bandsmen were triers. (The band had entered another contest at Bournville, where they had come fourth out of ten, the adjudicator admitting great difficulty in separating the bands).

The idea that the bandsmen were triers was taken up at the Annual Meeting and Dinner that was held at the *Black Horse* in Overend in January 1930. Mr. Hackett, in presenting the annual report, remarked *"The band began without a piece of brass and with no finances, and difficulties have been surmounted by steadfast plodding.*

The band is now uniformly clothed, and it has a good set of instruments and a snug little balance at the bank." The phrase "steadfast plodding" is, of course, a reference to the band's steady determination to succeed – not to the manner of its musical performance.

Ted Starling (later to be chairman of Halesowen Urban District Council), speaking at the same dinner, said that he thought that the band needed new instruments. The committee obviously took this advice to heart. In April, the band was back at the *Black Horse* playing at a sheep-roasting, for which tickets were sold at threepence each – in aid of the instrument fund.

Demise

There is not room here for a full history of the XLCR band. It played in Cradley during five decades. Amid changing times and tastes, interest from musicians and public alike began to decline in the post-war world, and in the 1960's the decline became steep. The XLCR is believed to have disbanded in or about 1968, about ten years after Jim Robinson's death.

The Cradley Band had played at carnivals and sheep-roastings, in parades and on bandstands, at church services and sacred concerts, and at sports and fêtes. It had played regularly on Armistice Day (and it had played at the unveiling of Cradley's war memorial). And throughout its existence it had supported a wide variety of local charities.

Jim Robins and his band brought pleasure – and pride – to Cradley. The band's demise is regrettable; its resurrection improbable.

Photographer unidentified

The XLCR Band – strangely un-uniformed – on the Oakley lorry in a Cradley Carnival in about 1947 (Ken Oakley is in the passenger seat). The lorry is turning out of Colley Gate into Colley Lane. Jim Robins (in the trilby) is standing with his back to the cab; William Smith is on his left with the bass euphonium. The flag behind William Smith is probably that of the band. The trombonist on the extreme right is Howard Clift. Its usual instrumentation at this time was: two or three trombones, five cornets, two horns, a tenor horn, two tenor and two baritone euphoniums, a bass euphonium and a drum.

A View from St. Pet

As you looked southwards from St. Peter's church tower in 1959, you could still see what had been Cradley's most striki
stack remained standing until 1960 or 1961. Its eventual demolition was carried out by the firm of Peter Scott (a forn
walls at the base of the stack were four feet thick.

Church Road has not changed very much: the Church Schools on the right, the row of terraced houses on the left fac
row of houses reads 'Harold Raybould, Complete House Furnisher'). The sign isn't there now.

The Liberal Club and *The Elms* (now demolished) stand to the left of the lower end of Colley Lane School's playing fie

Opposite the Liberal Club, the mouth of the narrow gully running from Colley Lane to Maple Tree Lane is visible. T
chainshop are discernible about an inch further to the left. The chainshop was demolished during December 1960 a

The vehicles parked together on the extreme left of the photograph are standing on the forecourt of the Blue Ball garag

Church Tower in 1959

dmark for almost forty years – the chimney stack of Beech Tree Colliery. The colliery closed in 1958, but the
yor of Halesowen); a Wolverhampton firm supplied the explosive expertise. Demolition was not a simple matter; the

schools, and the Baptist Chapel (the Sunday School at the time) are still there. (The sign on the gable end of the

school itself being hidden by the trees.

ilding to the left of the entrance to the gully was the office of Reece's Chainworks; the windows and chimneys of the
uary 1961.

lue Ball Lane.

Lawyer Homer, The Limes and the Labour Club

The solicitor, Thomas Homer, was a widower who lived with his two unmarried daughters at *The Limes* (below) at the junction of Colley Gate and Toys Lane. In 1927, Mr. Homer was in his 89th year but in remarkably robust health. Not only was he still a practising solicitor, but in fine weather he almost invariably walked to his office in Brierley Hill – and he sometimes walked back as well. Mr. Homer had been articled to another Cradley solicitor, Jeston Homfray of *The Grange,* and had been admitted as a solicitor in 1863. His firm, Thomas Homer and Son was a one-man firm, his son having pre-deceased him fifteen years previously. His other son was a doctor.

During his career, Mr. Homer had established a reputation for handling cases of damage to property through mining subsidence, and was generally credited with ensuring that property on the main road at Colley Gate was safeguarded from damage by mining – but how he achieved this does not appear to have been recorded. He was a capable advocate, and on the 7th March, 1927 he had appeared before the Brierley Hill bench in a licensing matter.

Alert and smartly dressed, healthy and active, Mr. Homer was one of Cradley's best known figures. Indeed, so robust and frisky does he seem to have been that one is half-inclined to believe that – but for the unfortunate accident that befell him on Sunday, 20th March, 1927 – he might have been practising yet.

A convivial gathering on a December afternoon in 1927 witnessed the formal conversion of *The Limes* into Cradley Labour Club. Wilfred Wellock, MP for Halesowen and Stourbridge presided over the gathering, and Charles Sitch, MP for Kingswinford, performed the opening ceremony. Alf Westwood made a speech, and the meeting concluded with two verses of the *Red Flag.*

The photograph was taken in 1968, when *The Limes* was demolished and the new Labour Club, visible in the background, was opened.

On that Sunday evening at about 9.15 p.m., his daughters – Sarah and Evelyn – heard a loud crash and, rushing out into the hall, they found their father lying at the foot of the stairs. What caused his fall remains unknown, but Mr. Homer suffered a fracture to the base of the skull. He died three days later, and at the inquest in the police station on the Thursday afternoon, the coroner (Mr. F. P. Evers) returned a verdict of accidental death.

Mr. Homer had spent the last evening of his life listening to the wireless (he would never have called it the radio), and it is surprising that he owned such a new-fangled gadget. In his office there was neither typewriter nor telephone.

His last conversation with his daughters had been on the subject of the China question (one of the political controversies of 1927 was the sending of British troops to Shanghai to protect British citizens caught in the Chinese civil war). Mr. Homer was a staunch Conservative, and his spirit must have been disturbed two months later when, at an auction at the *Talbot Hotel,* his old house was knocked down to Alf Westwood who paid £700 for it on behalf of Cradley Labour Party. After £300 had been spent on alterations (all the work being done by Cradley craftsmen) *The Limes* was opened as Cradley Labour Club on 17th December 1927. The present Labour Club straddles the former grounds not only of Thomas Homer but also of Frank Hipkiss, another prominent local Conservative: a teasing and continuing irony to be savoured or deplored, depending on which side of the political fence you stand.

Mr. Homer also owned – and developed – the land on the opposite corner of the Toys Lane – Colley Gate junction. He stipulated that no machinery should be installed in any building to be erected there. On the land over the road from his front gate stood Mr. Homer's orchard. Children used to peep longingly inside if they happened to be passing when John Shuck* – Mr. Homer's gardener – opened the gate to enter or leave the orchard. (Part of which is now the *Gate Inn* car-park)

Thomas Homer, *The Limes* – and the lime trees that once lined its boundary – have gone; it would be a shame if they were forgotten.

**John Shuck, a sidesman and former bellringer at St. Peter's Church, outlived his old employer by over six years. He died in October 1933, aged 87.*

Colley Gate during the winter of 1968-69. The new Labour Club wall is visible on the left. The Gate Inn car park marks the site of part of Thomas Homer's orchard. Percy Smith's shop *(see p.39)* *used to occupy the building on the nearside of the car park.*

Cradley Carnival

The annual carnival that was held in Cradley during the 1930's was no mere Saturday street parade; it was a communal upheaval. The idea of a carnival possibly grew from the successful 'gymkhana' that was held in June 1928 to raise funds for the extensive alterations to the Church School that were to be carried out later that year. The 'gymkhana' was essentially a fancy dress parade and procession, but on a fairly elaborate pattern. The climactic ceremony on Homer Hill Recreation Ground involved sports, sideshows, competitions, lorry-borne tableaux, the ducking of a witch (in fact, the witch was Tom Cox) and the 'crowning' of the Lord Mayor of Cradley. The part of the Lord Mayor was played by the Church School headmaster, George Raybould, who arrived in a brougham drawn by a hefty white cart-horse. Draped in Cradley chain (his badge of office) and responding to cries of 'Spake!' (he affected not to understand calls of 'Speech!'), Mr. Raybould promised 'free beer and no work for everybody'. The spectacle of a local headmaster disporting himself in this manner must have been a diverting one. Especially to his pupils.

Annual Event

In 1929, what was called 'the first annual Cradley carnival' was held, along similar lines to those of the previous year's gymkhana. It was in 1930 that the Carnival Committee really began to exercise its imagination. The committee was an offshoot of the Friendly Societies Parades Committee, which organised parades and street collections in aid of local hospitals and medical charities.

Although the carnival did not take place until July, the committee began its work in March. Regular committee meetings took place at various locations – the *Holly Bush, the Horse and Jockey, the White Horse* and other similar places. The committee was exclusively male.

Decorations

Extensive street decorations gave the first indication that a carnival was about to take place – a carnival, moreover, that was to be spread over a full week. The *County Express* reporter (probably Walter Pugh) was quite carried away by the scene in the streets:

> '. . . . *walking or riding down the High Street, one was confronted by as gorgeous a display of colouring as has been seen in any of the surrounding districts* (Stourbridge, Lye and Cradley

Photo: Nova Studios, Stourbridge

The 1930 Carnival procession included a Co-op. float under the title of *Dividend Day*. This is almost certainly that float. The girl in glasses third from the left (under the *£10,600* notice) is Ethel Cartwright. Behind her in the bowler hat is Jim Willetts. Marie Worton is holding the *Help the Hospitals* notice, and Joyce Goodwin and Marjorie Growcott are seventh and eighth from the left on the front row. Bernice Willetts is in the broad-brimmed straw hat on the back row, with Lily Heath in the tam o' shanter next to her. Emily Wood is on the extreme right of the back row, with her brother Jim in front of her.

Heath, for example, all held carnivals). *The delightful effect is heightened by some of the business premises being illuminated with electric fairy lights. Even the poorest of the houses have been enlivened with flags and streamers and greenery, not only along the main streets but all the side streets . . .'*

Each evening during carnival week, past all these trimmings strolled young men and women in fancy dress – all of them *'. . . enveloped from head to foot, and bearing a query (?) mark on their chests . . . parading the streets from Colley Gate to the Stour bridge . . . the passer-by is unable to recognise any of them.'*

Roast Mutton

Another nightly feature of carnival week was sheep-roasting, beginning on Monday with roastings at the *Why Not?* and the *Duke William*. Other roastings subsequently took place at *The Fish, White Lion, Holly Bush, Old Crown, White Horse, Maypole, Bridge Inn, Robin Hood* and *The Vine* in Two Gates. The last roasting took place on the Monday after the carnival week was over. Sheep, bread and fuel were provided by various local benefactors, and at each roasting the first cuts from the sheep were auctioned (over £1 was often paid for the first slice – little enough today but virtually a week's wages for many at the time).

Other Diversions

There was a treasure hunt in the front garden of the Vicarage; for threepence a go, you had a chance of winning a motor trip to Blackpool. There were whist drives, and on the Thursday evening there was a carnival dance at Colley Lane School – Billy Harbach was Master of Ceremonies. The Cradley Heath Male Voice Choir visited the parish – a touch of culture, perhaps, to relieve the frivolity. Many shopkeepers organised their own competitions (and gave their own prizes).

On the Wednesday there was what was called a jazz-band contest – a colourful and animated occasion to judge by the press report – but not including any jazz in the real meaning of the word (the bands probably featured the massed drum-beating and – especially – kazoo-blowing that comprise the fare provided by such bands today). The contest was held in Bert Mapp's field in Tanhouse Lane. Over twenty bands took part.

Photo: Nova Studios, Stourbridge

A float from the carnival in 1932. Back row (left to right): Betty Gauden, Edith Hadley, Cynthia Aston, Marie Worton. Front row: Mary Lee, Edna Homer, Della Greaves, Doris Knowles. The theme was suggested by a Dutch operetta called ***Jan of Windmill Land****, which had been performed by members of Providence Methodist Sunday School and Girls' Guild in the previous January. The float and the windmill were constructed by Sam Gauden and his son, Vernon.*

Photographer unidentified

Dressed for carnival in the 1930's (and note the contrasting dress of the two old ladies in the background). The flowery-trousered figure on the left remains unidentified. The others (from the left) are Beatrice Gillam, Ivy Gill and Gladys Hill. An interesting feature of the photograph is the old bandstand – and what appear to be the hanging gardens of Cradley. The object in Gladys Hill's left hand is presumably a collecting box, not a handbag. The photograph was taken near the bottom of the road that now leads to Cradley High School.

The Procession

There were some twenty-five floats in the procession, as well as innumerable pedestrians in all kinds of fancy dress, and many incidental diversions such as Red Indians on horseback, and a model steamroller mounted on the frame of a bicycle.

A huge crowd (and twenty jazz bands at full volume) assembled at Homer Hill to see the judges choose the best float, and to award various prizes for costumes. The winning float was that of Sheet Iron Workers Ltd., Cradley: *'The sides of the lorry were decorated with straw to a depth of about two feet, and quite a natural touch was provided by the insertion of poppies. When the sun shone and a slight breeze sprang up, the tableau with its waving grain and rocking poppies was extremely attractive . . . . . "*

The judging was completed by 4.30 p.m. when, headed by Cradley XLCR band, the procession wound its way through Cradley – Colley Lane, High Street, Lyde Green, Netherend Lane, Park Lane, Park Road, Colley Gate, Toys Lane, Two Gates, Beech Tree Colliery – then back along Two Gates, Two Gates Lane, Windmill Hill, Furlong Lane, Banners Lane, Colman Hill, Windmill Hill and Colley Gate.

In the words of the *County Express, "A really brilliant procession, undoubtedly the largest and most spectacular ever witnessed in Cradley, brought Carnival Week to a fitting close on Saturday. It is estimated that at least 2,000 persons took some part in this appropriate climax to a week of great endeavour . . . "*

Cricket and Tennis

On Thursday of Carnival Week a charity cricket match was played between Harper and Moore (the brickworks in Park Road) and Percy Smith's XI. The match was played on Harper and Moore's ground (the old Colley Gate ground behind the Talbot Hotel), and was won by Percy Smith's XI by thirteen runs. Vernon Clifton scored 27 for the winners, and Bert Bowen *' . . . the promising young Stourbridge batsman, showed excellent defence and some good scoring strokes.'* But perhaps the most interesting feature of the game was the appearance of a young Eric Hollies (the future Warwickshire and England player) as a guest for Harper and Moore, and of his father, Will Hollies (the last lob bowler to play in the Birmingham League) for Percy Smith.

The semi-finals – and probably the final – of the tennis tournament were played on Harold Willetts' court in the grounds of Colman Hill House. The games were umpired by a representative of Messrs. Dunlop & Co. who gave the score pads and provided the balls at a special rate.

The winners were Mr. R. Botwood and Miss Perry from Stourbridge tennis club. After what the *County Express* described as *'three exhilarating sets'* they beat Glen Reece and Winnie Bloomer, who appeared under the flag of Old Hill Cricket and Tennis Club. Mrs. Grice of Colman Hill presented the cups to the winners, and £14 1sh. 4d. was raised for carnival funds.

Distribution

On the 30th July, the Carnival Committee met in the Conservative Club under the chairmanship of Frank Hipkiss to hear how much money had been raised. The total to that date was £340 6sh. 5d., of which £170 15sh. 2d. had been raised by street collections. To put these sums into perspective, three years earlier *The Limes* – a detached house of reasonable size (see p. 26) – had sold for £700 at auction. There was more money to come, including small sums from whist drives at both Labour and Liberal Clubs, and the final total approached £400.

After lengthy discussion, the committee decided to distribute about one third of the money immediately. Apart from a gift of £10 to the Cradley Nursing Association (which employed Cradley's District Nurse) the money was divided among seven local hospitals.

Communal Effort

As a manifestation of community spirit, the Carnival of 1930 speaks for itself. Furthermore, the regular raising of money for local hospitals (and other events than carnivals were organised for this purpose) probably made people feel more involved with their local hospitals than they do today.

It is impossible to name all those who helped in the organisation of the 1930 Carnival but (though it seems invidious to select just a few individuals) it might be appropriate – for the record – to name the leading committee members:–

General Committee: Chairman, Mr. Frank Hipkiss; Vice-Chairman, Mr. Albert Hodgetts; Hon. Secretary, Mr. W. Jones.

Carnival Committee: Chairman and organiser, Mr. J. Smith; Vice-Chairman, Mr. W. Goode; Joint Secretaries, Mr. W. Jones and Mr. J. C. Bastable.

The carnivals were resumed after the Second World War, but by the mid-1950's, with public enthusiasm in steep decline, they were – by now shadows of their old selves – finally abandoned.

Photographer unidentified

The lorry of J. S. Rock and Sons coming down Windmill Hill in a carnival procession in the 1930's. Note the collecting box carried by the woman on the running board.

Colman Hill House

Photographer unidentified

Colman Hill House (above) which stood in wooded grounds in the angle of Colman Hill and Banners Lane, was a feature of the local landscape that Cradley could ill afford to lose. It was of no great architectural distinction, but by its size – as well as by the area of its grounds – it added variety and a touch of class to the parochial scene. It is quite possible that the building as shown in the photograph does not show Colman Hill House as it originally appeared. The gable-end on the left is obviously taller than the other two, and this suggests later alteration or extension to the original building. The drip-moulding (the dark 'brackets' above the windows) suggest the early nineteenth century, but a later one could easily have been installed to match earlier ones. The unmatching bay windows also suggest later addition; in fact it is possible that neither featured in the original building.

The ground's many mature trees attracted enough wild birds to make the dawn chorus in Colman Hill memorable. But Colman Hill House had more to offer the community than birdsong. Its tennis court (one of the net-posts of which is visible in the photograph) was one of those used in the annual carnival tennis tournament, and garden parties were frequently held in its grounds. The garden party that was in progress when the above photograph was taken was in aid of St. Peter's Church in 1946.

For much of the nineteenth century, the house seems to have been occupied by the New British Iron Company – probably as a residence for senior staff – and at some time around the turn of the century, it became a home for female alcoholics. It will still be remembered by some as the home of Herman Garratt who had previously lived at Holloway House in Drews Holloway. Mr. Garratt was a member of Garratt's Ltd., Firebrick Manufacturers of Corngreaves, and of Stourbridge Old Wharf Saw Mills Ltd. He died, aged 59, on 24th October 1928, leaving a widow, a daughter and three sons. Though the family apparently all lived at home, Colman Hill House was sold after Herman Garratt's death.

Prospective purchasers were invited to apply to W. H. Chapman at Corngreaves Offices, Cradley Heath (this was probably the same W. H. Chapman who was at the time Chairman of Cradley School Managers, and a well-known figure in the parish).

Suitable applications were obviously not forthcoming, because in January 1929, Colman Hill House was advertised for sale by public auction (Leslie Tibbetts being the auctioneer). The house was described in adver-

Photographer unidentified

Above: A back view of Colman Hill House, photographed by one of the Willetts family.

Left: Harold Willetts (1884 – 1972), the last owner of Colman Hill House.

tisements in the following terms: " . . . *freehold commodious residence, standing in an elevated position in its own grounds (about 5¾ acres) . . 8 bedrooms . . 2 bathrooms . . 3 reception rooms . . billiard room . . cellaring, etc.*"

The house was bought by Harold Willetts who lived there until September 1964, when house and grounds were sold for development. Harold Willetts was managing director of Charles Willetts Jnr. Ltd., a firm which had been founded by his father. He also succeeded his father as organist at Cradley Baptist Chapel, in which post Charles Willetts served for 25 years, and Harold for over 50 years. Harold Willetts also installed an organ in the lounge of Colman Hill House.

Photo: Betty Parsons

Two more demolished houses: the Jones family's cottage in Shelton Lane (left), photographed about 1956. It stood just above the junction with Stourdell Road. Linton House (right), stood in its own grounds at the top of Drews Holloway, just below its junction with Beecher Road. Another of the Cradley houses that had its own tennis court, it was owned by (among others) the chain manufacturer Henry Reece – until his death in 1924 – and in its later days by Gilbert Lee, the Clerk to the Justices at Old Hill.

Colley Lane School

Photographer unidentified

Above: Colley Lane Junior School Staff in June 1950. Back row (left to right): Geoff Hodgetts, Matthew Wadham, Jack Shakespeare (headmaster), Wilf Cox, Ben Kirton. Front row: Ivy Shaw, Gwladys Morris, Ellen Jones, Maisie Higgs, Betty Corcoran.

★ ★ ★ ★

Above right: The staff of Colley Lane Boys' School in 1928 or 1929. Back row (left to right): Unidentified, Walter Hodgetts, Charles Westwood, Bill Tibbetts, Unidentified, Mr. Drayton, Norman Bird, Vernon Hodgetts. Front row: Sim Wharton (in his wing collar but – unusually – without his spats), Edith Coley, Tom Allchurch (headmaster), Tolie Duffett, Francis Hickman.

Bill Tibbetts died aged only twenty-four in October 1929. He had been on the staff for eighteen months. Horace Goodwin, who was in Bill Tibbetts' class at the time of his death, remembers that he was replaced by Jack Shakespeare. (Jack Shakespeare had received his Diploma in Education from Birmingham University in 1927. He was probably a temporary replacement for Bill Tibbetts, as he later taught at Hill and Cakemore before returning to Colley Lane as headmaster just before the war). Mr. Goodwin has also attached each named teacher to his or her class, leaving no class unaccounted for. It therefore seems likely that the two unidentified teachers were student-teachers from a local training college – a possibility rendered more likely by the fact that they both have identical badges on their blazers. (Saltley College – Tom Allchurch's old college – is a possibility).

Tom Allchurch also died prematurely in 1934. Walter Hodgetts was later to be a wartime Mayor of Halesowen

★ ★ ★ ★

Below right: Standard 1 of Colley Lane Boys in 1930. Back row (left to right): Alf Stokes, Charles Batham, Jack Taylor, Bert Raybould, Frank Clifton, Richard Wheelwright, Fred Townsend, Douglas Shilvock, Lilian Webster; Second row: Jack Wellings, Ronnie Mills, Tom Bate, Alf Robinson, George Wood, Ashley Neale, Ben Nock, Dennis Taylor, Gerald Cox, Ken Oakley; Third row: Geoffrey Edge, Ernie Edmonds, Moses Crewe, Fred Wood, Clifford Smith, John Homer, Harold Goodwin, Frank Pearson, Godfrey Fradgley; Fourth row: John Carradine, Joe James, Wesley Beasley, Albert Guest, Albert Crampton, Jack Harbach, Sydney Hill; Front row: Tom Beasley, Bob Tate, Vernon Cox, George Kinsley, Don Bevan, Walter Priest.

Lilian Webster was subsequently Mrs. Jack Shakespeare.

– Staff and Pupils

Photographer unidentified

Photographer unidentified

Colley Lane Infants' School Staff – 1950

Photographer unidentified

Back row (left to right): Sheila Griffiths, Marjorie Meredith, Beatrice Byng (school secretary); Front row: Muriel Brett Young, Minnie Kitchen, Alice Meredith, Olive Willetts (headmistress), Dilys Stonebridge, Kathleen Jones. Muriel Brett Young was half-sister of the Halesowen-born novelist, Francis Brett Young. Homer Hill Secondary Modern School (now Cradley High School) is clearly visible in the background, though the buildings have, of course, now been replaced.

Reece's Chainworks in Colley Lane

Photographer unidentified

Henry Reece died in July 1924, and his son took over the business. A likely date for this photograph is 1930 – or thereabouts. Back row (left to right): Unidentified, Sam Bate, John Bate, Harry Willetts, Sam Willetts, Wesley Robinson, Bill Fowkes. Front row: David Deeley, Alf Slater, Unidentified, Glen Reece, (the next three men are unidentified), Arthur Cox.

Lyde Green and Bridge Street

Photographer unidentified

Lyde Green (above) near its junction with Bridge Street and what was then Cradley High Street. The photograph was published in the *Methodist Gazette* in 1895. The Wesleyan Chapel is still there, as is the house next to it – which was once the home of the minister and, later, the caretaker. The nearer houses have been demolished.

Bridge Street as it looked in the 1960's. The grocer's shop on the corner of Mill Street, which was run for many years by the Blunts, and later by Mrs. Alfred Woodhouse, has now been demolished. The bulky and uncompromising brick building remains.

A Cradley Choir

Photo: W. R. Bebb Jones, Stourbridge.

St. Katherine's choir, probably in 1938. Back row (left to right): Bert Blunt (sidesman), Sam Worton, Frank Knowles, Harry Barber, Edgar Williams, Garnett Harris, Jim Dunlop, Wilf Overton, Vernon Clifton (organist and choirmaster), Percy Smith, Howard Dunlop, Arthur Trevis, Luther Etherington, Harry Cox. Front row: Ruth Bullingham, Madge Pugh, Miriam Knowles, Ivy Dunlop, Doris Pugh, Rev. Ernest Toulouse (vicar of Cradley), Rev. Wallace Cox (curate), Vera Bullingham, Mabel Clifton, Winnie Pugh, Lilian Woodall, Eileen Forrest, Megan Beasley.

Two Old Choristers

It is perhaps unfair to select particular choristers for special mention, but a few words at least must be said about Luther Etherington and Harry Cox. The former, in his younger days, was apt to disturb neighbours with his practice on the bugle – that instrument being perhaps a legacy of his army days, during which he served in the Boer War. Luther Etherington also had a career in amateur dramatics, and a fascinating glimpse of this career survives in the shape of a programme of an entertainment called *Mrs. Jarley's Waxworks** that was presented at Whitley Memorial School, Cradley Heath in April 1926. The performance consisted of a series of sketches under the direction of Mrs. William Herald, the wife of the Cradley curate. Luther took part in three of these sketches, playing successively Sleeping Beauty, a Gypsy King and John Bull. The last-named part (in which he was accompanied by Miss Alice Oliver as Britannia) perhaps suited him best.

Harry Cox, mostly remembered now as the licensee of the *Round of Beef,* had some local reputation as a cricketer in his earlier days. He played for Colley Gate, and as a batsman he believed in taking the attack to the bowler. If you can believe ancient legend, Harry – once he had his eye in – would take two or three steps out of his crease, and swing his bat through an arc of about 270 degrees, accompanying the stroke with a loud and unchorister-like shout of "Osher!" (This might, of course, have been an abbreviation of 'Hosannah!'. But it seems unlikely).

A Memorable Evening

Harry Cox sometimes combined the duties of chorister and licensee, as he did, for instance, on the evening of Thursday, 9th January, 1930, when he and his wife hosted the choir's annual dinner at the *Round of Beef.* It was a convivial evening. Dinner was eaten, toasts were drunk, and then chairs were pushed back and legs stretched out as the diners prepared to enjoy the entertainment.

Luther Etherington sang *Absent* and *Queen of My Heart;* Mr. Bowen and Vernon Clifton sang the duet *Larboard Watch;* and Walter Pugh and Percy Smith sang *Watchman, What of the Night?* and *Excelsior.* The full choir also took part, singing the glees *Sweet and Low, In Absence, Comrades in Arms* and *Little Tommy Went a-Fishing.* The accompaniments were shared by Vernon Clifton and Harry Cox, and the evening ended with an ensemble rendering of *God Save the King.*

There is no record that the company, with its appetite satisfied and its spirits lifted, left behind the embers of a blazing fire, and stepped outside and found its way home through a starry, frosty night. But one can hope that it did.

**For "Jarleys Waxworks" see "The Old Curiosity Shop" by Charles Dickens.*

– And a Memorable Barber

Another chorister, Percy Smith, was well-known for his pleasant bass voice, which was frequently heard in concerts in pubs and clubs – singing solos and duets – as well as in the St. Kath's choir. Percy was also well-known as chairman of the Cradley Branch of the British Legion, as the organiser of annual charity cricket and football matches, and even as an umbrella-mender. But above all else he was known as a barber. In his pursuit of this occupation he was also the permanent chairman of a continuing public discussion group comprising Percy's clientele at any given moment.

The Shop

Percy's shop was in Colley Gate, almost opposite its junction with Toys Lane (the building is still there). Inside, it had a gloomy, rather furtive atmosphere that added a hint of adventure to the mundane experience of having your hair cut. As you walked past the counter in the outer shop (where tobacco and confectionery were sold), you found yourself walking down a slight slope towards an inner door. You felt that you ought to knock. Did you need to know a password?

As you walked through the doorway, you faced a large mirror on the opposite wall. On the mirror there were stickers that read *'Use Top Mill Snuff'* and *'Singeing Promotes the Growth of the Hair'* (Percy used to carry out this operation with a comb and a long, lighted taper). In front of the mirror were two barber's chairs, side by side.

Customers on wooden chairs lined the other three walls, and an iron stove stood in the centre of the room. In winter, the stove and the exclusively masculine clientele made you feel that you were entering a barber's shop in some gold-rush town in the Yukon. (Women, it must be admitted, only entered the barber's shop in their role as guardians of infant sons; they always looked self-conscious and uneasy, like trespassers).

The Method

As a barber, Percy was restless and energetic. He was notable for his ability to shave one customer and cut the hair of another almost simultaneously. As they sat side by side, Percy, in his long, brown barber's coat, would leave one of them lathered to the eyebrows while he turned and completed the preliminary snipping of the other. Thus alternating between the two, Percy circled each chair as he worked. Occasionally, with his knees slightly bent and his scissors still snipping or his cut-throat razor poised, he would take a step back to admire his handywork and pick his spot for the next strike.

The Discussion

All the time, Percy kept an ear open to the exchange of views and information (well, yes, sometimes it was gossip) that was going on around him. Like all good chairmen, he did not take part in the discussion. He was perfectly armed to deal with any statement made to him by any customer, no matter how hot the debate. If the statement could be answered merely by an acknowledgment that he had heard and understood it, Percy simply said 'Ar'. If the statement contained information or opinion of an unexpected or controversial nature, Percy invariably replied 'Gerrout!' In either case, he had preserved his essential neutrality.

Diversion was frequently provided by the arrival of a customer in the outer shop. In response to the bell, Percy would stop barbering, hurdle the outstretched legs of his patrons, brush aside the curtain that hung across the doorway to the shop, and serve the customer. Then, with another rapidly executed series of hops, skips and jumps, Percy would return to his proper concerns. If, when the bell rang, Percy was deeply involved in his work (or if the discussion was at a particularly interesting point) Percy invariably shouted 'Wanya want?' If the request seemed merely frivolous or vexatious, he simply shouted in reply 'We'n got none.'

The conversation was composed of endless variations on the themes of local news, sport (with special reference to the fortunes of local football clubs) and politics. The ever-changing congregation in Percy's shop reflected in its talk the strains and stresses, moods and humours of the larger community outside. But its manner was generally leisurely, and a newcomer could slip into the conversation as easily as a jazz musician into a jam session, make his contribution to the discussion, and leave afterwards with the feeling of having enjoyed a convivial meeting, made a useful contribution to social intercourse, and hardly conscious of having had his hair cut.

Left: Percy Smith in yet another rôle. The cap-badge suggests the South Staffordshire Regiment. The identity of the photographer is not known.

Cradley below St. Peter's Church (1959-1961)

Above left: The rooftops of High Street and – in the background – New Street, photographed in about 1959. The bay windows of the half-demolished *Fish Inn* are on the right, next to Sam and Ken Willetts' bakery. Below the bakery are the *Holly Bush* and the old *Robin Hood Inn,* the latter then leading a more decorous existence as a mission hall.

Top right: The three ladies on the step were photographed in New Street at about the same period.

Bottom right: This photograph, also taken in the late 1950's, shows Victoria Street, which ran down to meet the lower end of New Street. The lady on the left is Jean Bloomer.

The view (above) from St. Peter's church tower, looking towards Cradley Heath in the late 1950's. The white-painted side wall of the *Bridge Inn,* towards the lower end of Bridge Street, is visible on the left. The buildings of Little Hill and the lower part of High Street are huddled together in the foreground, with the chainworks of Jones and Lloyd prominent on the left (the firm's 'top shop' and offices were at the top of the High Street).

On the Cradley Heath side of the bridge over the Stour are the *Jolly Collier* (to the right of the road and opposite the gasworks), and the as yet undeveloped Porter's Field.

Photo: John Billingham

The Jones and Lloyd chainshop from ground-level in 1961. In the background the junction of High Street, Lyde Green and Bridge Street. (This is the only photograph in the booklet that was originally in colour).

Cradley High Street

Cradley High Street has a peaceful, almost somnolent, air on a quiet summer afternoon in 1958. It had known more exciting times – at least in the Roaring Twenties. In October 1925, for instance, there was a fire in Millward's ('Tink's') shop. Nearby roadmenders rushed to help, the fire brigade was summoned, and a police sergeant and two constables arrived. The shop was described in the *County Express* as *'a kind of general household stores, containing much that is highly inflammable.* The *County* explained the dramatic climax of the incident: *'The greatest excitement prevailed with regard to the removal of a paraffin tank.'* Disaster was avoided; the fire-brigade did not even have to run out a hose.

In December of the same year, a police constable posing as a tailor uncovered an illegal football sweep in the *Fish Inn.* Landlord Tommy North was playing 'Don' (a card game) for money with some of his customers, and the whole episode cost him £14 13sh (fines and costs) before Stourbridge magistrates.

The most spectacular disaster happened in November 1928, when a horse attached to a bread van bolted in Ladysmith Road, turned right into Maple Tree Lane and continued at the gallop down the High Street. On its way it damaged a mudguard on Walter Southall's van, and broke both shafts on a stationary horse-drawn cart belonging to Jones and Lloyd. Neither collision stopped the careering horse, which swung right into Little Hill (which is just beyond the lower bend in the photograph) and – finding itself in a dead-end – came to a standstill against the wall of Walter Williams' chainshop.

Earlier in the same decade, another horse had bolted through the plate glass window of Dentith's bread shop in the angle of the High Street/Little Hill junction. The horse had to be destroyed on the spot.

Cradley High Street in the 1920's, it seems, had something of the atmosphere of Dodge City half a century earlier.

The photograph: Ken Bradney's butcher's shop is under the awning on the right, with Wilf Williams' greengrocery on the far side of the step. The *Holly Bush* is immediately below Willetts' bakery, with the Cradley Pentecostal Mission (previously the *Robin Hood Inn*) on the opposite corner of New Street. The sign of the *White Horse* is just visible in the background.

The van is Ken Bradney's new Commer; the car that has just pulled away from the kerb is quite probably Rex Meredith's Austin 16.

Two Gates Lane

Like the other photographs on this page, the summer-evening shot (left) of Two Gates Lane, looking towards its junction with Windmill Hill, was taken in the early 1960's. The road sign – 'Halt at Major Road Ahead' – once such a familiar sight to drivers – now seems as quaint and remote a part of the motoring scene as cobbled streets, hand-signals and Leslie Hore-Belisha.

At the time, Cradley's gas-lamps were being replaced with electric ones. Outside the wine shop in the background, there was already an electric lamp (concealed in the photograph by the gas-lamp); its shadow is clearly visible across the pavement in front of the shop.

The Wine Shop

The wine shop was owned by William Gardner, and as you walked in you were likely to find him behind his counter facing you . . . . .

Originally a newsagent in Lye, Mr. Gardner's business expanded to include the newsagent's and the wine shop at the top of Windmill Hill, as well as wine shops in Lye and Stourbridge. He lived in *Fairview* – Charles Willetts' old house in Drews Holloway.

A generous friend of Providence Methodist Church, the Manse at the bottom of Highfield Road was a gift from him.

Another Junction

The view from the top of Furlong Lane (left). Several buildings on both sides of the road have since been demolished, including the *Duke William* (the bay-windowed building on the left, just above the Morris Minor) and the *British Arms,* which was on the opposite side just below it.

The buildings were demolished because they lay in the path of the proposed A458 relief road. The demolition seems to have been a little premature.

Two Shops in Windmill Hill

The Baker's

The photograph of Walter Holden's shop – bread, cakes, biscuits and confectionery – was taken in the middle or late 1920's. The lady in the doorway is Evelyn Beasley, of Colley Orchard, who worked behind the counter in the shop.

Photographer unidentified

★ ★ ★ ★

And the Shoe-Shop

Farther up the hill, on the same side, was Jewiss's shoe shop – though at the time the photograph was taken, the business was run by V. E. Stevens (Footwear). Violet Elsie Stevens was the sister of Frank and Alf Rudge, the builders. The window-display, designed to commemorate the Festival of Britain, makes the date (or at least, the year) of the photograph quite clear.

Photographer unidentified

Photographer unidentified

Errington's draper's shop, at the junction of Maple Tree Lane and Colley Gate, in the early 1950's, Wilf Homer is on the right; the man on the left is possibly Neri Beasley.

Photographer unidentified

Paul Homer's hardware store at the bottom of Blue Ball Lane. The date of the photograph is unknown – possibly about 1918. Paul Homer was followed in the business by his son, Ezra. By the end of 1931, Homer's shop and the house next door – as well as the Anvil Yard, which lay behind it – had all been demolished.

Photo: Paul Burgess

Beech Tree colliery, photographed from the direction of the Water-style in the mid-1950's.

Photographer unidentified

Only the two men at the front of this group, photographed at Beech Tree – probably in the 1930's – have been identified: Mr. Hayward (left) and Joe Willetts. Note the coal tubs on the left; they carried the coal under Oldnall Road and down the steep incline to pass under the Stourbridge Road to the railway sidings by Harper and Moore's brickyard.

Beech Tree Colliery

Beech Tree Colliery, Cradley's last pit, closed in the late summer of 1958. Coal had been first brought to the surface there in 1921, though a shaft had been sunk before 1900 by James Holcroft, whose name was still on the colliery's stack when it closed. Rival coal-owners brought up the mineral rights on one side, and the pit had to be developed 'outwards' along dwindling seams of poor quality coal.

Underground

The shaft at Beech Tree went down 180 yards, and the seams ran for about a mile. In its final days, the colliery employed 118 men and 27 pit-ponies. Ironically, working conditions had been considerably improved only a few months before the colliery closed, by the installation of coal-cutting machinery. Pit-head baths had been built some time before, but not until after the post-war nationalisation of the coal industry. The baths building is still standing, having been converted for use as a scout headquarters.

In its final year, the colliery produced 81,706 tons of coal. In its best year – 1947 – 87,000 tons were brought to the surface.

Water

The colliery had to be closed when water penetrated the surrounding clay and flooded the underground workings. All the cutting machinery at the coal-face was lost, and an estimated half a million tons of coal was left underground. The men were promised jobs elsewhere, but the average age of the men at Beech Tree was higher than in most pits, and George Jeavons (Beech Tree's last manager) thought that they might find it hard to adjust to different working conditions in other pits.

In Cradley, coal-mining now only survives in the recollections of an inevitably decreasing band of ex-colliers – men with vivid memories (and all too often, diseased lungs) who form a tenuous link with an increasingly distant and unremembered aspect of local life.

The Bath Meadow

The Bath Meadow (above) in about 1960. The house among the trees on the extreme left is Holloway House, which was for many years the home of H. J. Cox whose hardware store once stood on the corner of Foredraft Street almost opposite the *Round of Beef*. Just in front of Holloway House is Hilldene House, which was once the home of the baker Walter Holden, who kept three horses in the Bath Meadow. Among the houses visible in Colman Hill are those of Harry Cooper, a director of Jones and Lloyd (the Cradley chainmaking firm), the Colley Lane schoolmaster, Vernon Hodgetts, and George Raybould, who was headmaster of Cradley Church School.

The footpath across the field is shown on the 1843 tithe map (on which the Bath Meadow is called Bath Field). It was then in the possession of James Evers. The name "Bath' probably merely indicates that there is water nearby.

The Bath Meadow was once the unofficial recreation ground for boys at this end of the parish. The worn strip at the bottom left of the field marks the site of both football and cricket pitches; in winter, tobogganists used the slope at the top right of the field. On at least one occasion, in August 1930, the Bath Meadow was used for Overend Mission's Sunday School Treat.

Photo: Betty Parsons

The photograph of haymakers in the Bath Meadow has a pre-war look about it, but it was in fact taken in or about 1960. The remnants of Witley Colliery's spoil bank – and the engine house to the left of it – are visible in the background. The white square that is discernible on the right of the row of houses in Belle Vale is the sign that marked a Banks' off-licence. The haymakers are at the top of the toboggan slope.

The style at the top of the Bath Meadow, (right) photographed from Shelton Lane in the late 1950's, with the side of Harry Rock's house visible on the right. The photograph was taken into the sun; hence the white disc blotting out the top rung of the style.

Homer Hill

Photo: Landscape View Publishers, Market Harborough

Homer Hill Recreation Ground, probably photographed in the early 1960's. In June 1932, a sub-committee of Halesowen Council's Baths and Recreation Grounds Committee recommended the purchase of the following for Homer Hill Recreation Ground: one set of swings (four seats) – £22; one 'ocean wave' – £35; and one thirty foot slide – £43. Total – £100. And there they all are. The struts on the right are part of the frame work of the swings. Visible along Colley Lane are the Liberal Club (then still separate from its assembly room), *The Elms* and (extreme right) Colley Lane School.

Photo: Express & Star

Homer Hill Youth Club Football Team, photographed before a home game against Blackheath Wanderers on 19th January, 1952. The team, which played in the Halesowen Youth League (for under-21 sides), was based at Homer Hill (now Cradley High) School, where its home matches were held. *Back row (left to right): Roy 'Tubby' Woodhouse, Haydn Briggs, Gerald Meyer, Peter Barnsley, Ken Cox, – Smith, Wilf Willetts, George Hughes (manager). Front row: Ron Priest, Geoffrey Green, Fred Hughes, Raymond Heath, Don Hill.*

Images from the 1960's

Silhouettes at St. Peter's . . . . . .

. . . . . . and a window in Two Gates

Where to Shop in the early 1930's

QUALITY, ATTENTION, AND MONEY SAVED

Shop in COLLEY GATE

AND WINDMILL HILL.

BY SHOPPING LOCALLY.

May we have Your Enquiries FOR

GROCERIES & PROVISIONS?

B. F. SOUTHALL,

COLLEY GATE.

Tel.: 6153 CRADLEY.

276

HOLLOWAY'S

FOR

HARDWARE

AND

FURNITURE.

— SPECIAL —

GARDEN SPADES

FROM 2/- EACH.

'Phone: 6115 and at Halesowen 141.

277

BIG REDUCTIONS.

Save as you Spend by getting your

GROCERIES & PROVISIONS

FROM

J. A. ADAMS,

38, FURLONG LANE,

COLLEY GATE,

'PHONE 6048.

274

WHEN SHOPPING AT COLLEY GATE

CALL AT

HAROLD ROPER'S

WINDMILL HILL.

FRESH FRUIT AND VEGETABLES DAILY.

CIVILITY IS OUR MOTTO.

271

HOLDEN'S

BREAD

THE BEST

BY TEST.

270

H. A. Woodall & Son,

for

SHIRTS

from 5/11 to 10/6

FLANNELS

from 10/6 to 21/-

FOR THE BEST GENUINE

Home Baked BREAD

You cannot beat

F. HEAD,

BEECHER BAKERY.

Made from Best Quality Flour only.

— ALSO —

TUROG,

THE BREAD OF EALTH.

PLEASE SEND FOR SAMPLE.

'PHONE 6469.

278

OUR ELECTRICAL INSTALLATIONS

ARE OF THE SAME HIGH QUALITY AS OUR WELL-KNOWN

SANITARY AND DECORATING WORK.

ADDRESS YOUR INQUIRIES TO

S. GAUDEN,

A.M. INST. B.E.

Phone: 6372 CRADLEY.

272

THE NOTED SHOP FOR QUALITY.

W. & J. DUNN

GROCERS, BAKERS & PROVISION MERCHANTS,

WINDMILL HILL STORES

'Phone: 6326 CRADLEY HEATH

OUR VANS ARE AT YOUR SERVICE

WEDDING & BIRTHDAY CAKES

MADE TO ORDER.

WE MAKE ALLISON'S BREAD

M. GARDENER,

Newsagent, Stationer and Wholesale Tobacconist.

ECONOMISE BY TRYING OUR

LOOSE SHAGS,

Black and Brown.

THICK AND THIN

TWIST.

ALSO

CIGARETTE TOBACCO

at 8d. per oz.

275

TRY US FOR

MOTOR TYRES.

Choose what make of Tyre you like best and we will give you

15% OFF LIST PRICE.

Specialists in WIRELESS BATTERIES.

Guarantees Given on Every Sale.

THOMPSON & Co.,

BEECHER GARAGE,

CRADLEY, STAFFS.

'PHONE 6454.

273

B. E. ERRINGTON,

BRADFORD HOUSE.

For RELIABLE DRAPERY at the Lowest Prices.

NEW STOCK OF THE FAMOUS

"BEAR BRAND" HOSE.

Smartest Shades and Longest W...

Popular Prices:

1/11½, 2/11, 3/11.

– from the "County Express"